A JOURNEY

A JOURNEY

DR PHIL CUMMINS

*For Brian and James and
Oliver and Brian*

Acknowledgements

I am very grateful for all of the family, friends and colleagues who have helped with this little book.

Dr Ian Lambert put the idea into my head, while Matthew Azzalin, Dr Hugh Chilton, Benjamin Cooper, Oliver Cummins, Dr Rohma Newman Cummins, Adriano Di Prato, Jack Pannell, Kyle Porter and Paul Vickers all helped bring it to life in various ways.

Alicia Cohen, Rica Dearman, Tess McCabe and the team from Amba Press have been wonderful, as ever – the best in the business.

Connecting and collaborating with my niece, Maia Jelavic, has been a joy.

And, in particular, Ms Julie Gillick OAM has been a wonderful reader and provocateur whose influence has shaped the story, much as her friendship and leadership have played an important role in shaping who I am.

Published in 2025 by Amba Press, Melbourne, Australia
www.ambapress.com.au

Cover design: Tess McCabe
Illustrations: Dr Brian Patrick Cummins and Maia Jelavic
Internal design: Amba Press
Editor: Rica Dearman

ISBN: 9781923403123 (pbk)
ISBN: 9781923403130 (ebk)

A catalogue record for this book is available from the National Library of Australia.

Contents

Prologue
Trust

Come with me, the man said.

Why? the boy replied.

We have a journey to take together. It's important. It will take some time.

Ah, but I have other plans.

They will need to wait. We need to do this together.

I see. I suppose we can.

Yes.

Where are we going?

Out there. We won't be coming back for some time. But we'll be back.

OK. Why are we going?

We have a thing to do. An important thing. You'll see.

Ah, OK. I'm not sure I do see.

But you can and you will. Everything that has come before it has prepared you for what must be done. Go and pack.

Will it be like other journeys we have taken?

Most likely. But also not. You will see. As much as it can be known, you already know this thing that must be done.

What does that mean? What will we be doing?

What have you done before? Use your memory. See back to what I've taught you and what you've seen me do before. What needs to be done? Use your eyes. See through to what's out there right now in the foreground and in the distance. What might be done next? Use your imagination. See forward to where we might go, whom we might meet and what might happen.

What should I bring?

You won't need much. Just bring what's essential.

How do I know what's essential?

You know already what's essential. Bring what you need. Don't weigh yourself down. Where we're going, you'll need what's essential to do what's essential. You'll carry it all yourself, so pack enough and no more.

Ah! What's enough?

I have answered this question many times before. You know already what is 'enough and no more'. You'll need layers you can take off and on. And something warm. Choose for fit and strength over fashion. You'll look good if you're comfortable in yourself and well prepared. And bring your book and a pen. I'll bring salt for flavour.

Of course. Will it be hard?

Yes. But not all of it. So, make sure you include one thing that's just for fun. A man's got to have some fun. Life is not all hard work and struggle.

How do you know so much? How do you know these things?

What I know and how I learned it are gifts that were passed on to me. I was taught and I learned. I asked and was answered. I listened well on occasion, but mostly not. I read and I studied. I wandered. And I wondered. I did much. I made many mistakes. I still make many mistakes.

If I have learned and know something that is needed, I will share this knowledge with you, boy. If I have become something of worth, I will also share this value with you. I ask you to come with me now and tell me what you need as we go so that I might give you what I can along the way. And I ask you to do the same for me. This is the good and right way to do it.

How do you know what's good? How do you know you're right?

I know what I know. You must judge for yourself what is good and right. You must also judge for yourself what I have and have become, and of what value I am to you in deciding what is good and right. That is your choice.

We have talked enough now, boy. So, look inside and beyond yourself, and see what we must do. And go and pack your things. No time to waste. See you shortly.

OK. Let's do this.

REFLECTION

1. What does it mean to trust someone? Do you trust yourself? Do other people trust you?

2. How well do you need to know someone before you trust them? What does it feel like when you are trusted, and you trust someone in return?

3. What gifts does trust bring? What burdens does trust bring? Can you trust too little? Can you trust too much?

4. Why do we need trust in our lives? Why must trust be earned?

NOTES

Part 1
Belonging

What is this place, old man? I've never seen anything like it before.

It is a special place.

What makes it special?

It is unlike anything else you have ever seen.

So, it is special because it is different?

Yes, but that does not give it all of its value. Because, in most respects, it is just like any other place. There is air, there is ground, there is light, there is water. There are living things all around it.

So, it is special because it is the same?

It is special because it is both the same and different. That is its character.

What do you mean by its character?

Its character is how it holds its place in the world. It is its being and its becoming. It does not stand still. It is always changing. And, so, it has a story of its yesterday, and its today, and its tomorrow.

The things that are in and of this place came to be here as part of this story. Each thing makes up part of the story and gives it part of its value, but together all of these things create a value that goes beyond themselves. This place, then, is both part and whole.

The part and whole of this place can help you, me, us to feel as though we belong here. It can help us to test out what might be possible for us. It can help us to choose to do good and right with this potential. In this way, the character of this place can help us to grow in our own character. Perhaps this is why it is most special to us.

In this manner, however, it is like any other place in the world. It might feel special in the moment because it is new and wonderful, and we can wander in it as though we had never experienced life fully before. But when we leave it, and leave we must in due course, what we take from it we will carry forward into every other place of our lives, both those that we know well and those we do not yet. Every place can be like this for us, if we allow it to be. If we can find its value.

Does that depend on us?

It does and it doesn't.

I knew you'd say something like that.

Ha! Of course.

Perhaps it's because there's something inside us that is growing and becoming while the world and all that's in it are doing the same.

It's hard to know whether it's you or what's around you that matters the most. Maybe that's because everything matters. But then, perhaps nothing matters.

> *Perhaps everything matters, but not as much as we think it does. Perhaps everything matters but in different amounts at different times.*

Perhaps you're learning something here.

> *Perhaps I might learn more somewhere else.*

Perhaps you might. Or not. Every place is special or not. Every one of us is special or not. Or perhaps it's not 'or' but 'and'. Special and not.

> *And now you're doing it again.*

Doing what?

> *Giving answers that are more like questions. Or at least leaving me asking more questions than before.*

Is that a good thing?

> *You talk about 'wonder and wander'. I like that.*

Yes. So, do I. But you can't always do that.

> *I know that already. It's hard to find the space to wonder and wander. There's so much to do, so many places to go, so many things to see, so much to create. And then, sometimes, it's just all too much and I don't want any of it. I just want to sit and do nothing. Or do something that takes away from nothing. Something that destroys. Just for the sake of it.*

We all have that potential in us. Each of us can be a cause of hope and despair. That's why we need to work out what is good and right. That's why we need to figure out what it is that we are meant to do, how we might best go about this, and then go and do it. That's our way of contributing to what is good and right.

But that's hard.

Yes.

You often say, 'hard is good'.

Yes.

I think that sometimes it can all be too hard.

Yes. And no.

You're doing it again, old man.

Perhaps I am. If it's hard, it's hard. It is what it is. It still has to be done. How you react to it is different from what it is. Too hard? Not hard enough? It depends on the task at hand and your willingness to do what's right to get it done.

You have to step back from yourself to see beyond your feelings to know what is right and what might be done about this, boy. That's never easy and it takes time – more time than you'd care to give to it. And yet you also have to look into yourself to know what is right. It's got to feel right as well as be right. Otherwise, it won't work for you, even though it might be right for everyone else.

But you always tend towards what's hard. And you forget to have fun.

And you tend towards what's not. And you try to have too much fun.

> *Yes. And no.*

Perhaps.

> *If it's too hard, too much, then there's no wonder. There's no wander either. There's only the work. And there's no beauty in the work. I think that when we wonder and when we wander, we're trying to find what is rare and beautiful.*

Sometimes we might find beauty in that way. That's a special thing. Yes, it is. There's always the work. That's also beautiful.

> *But the work gets in the way of the wonder. And it stops you from wandering. It stops you from finding what's truly beautiful.*

Maybe you need to wander between the wonder and the work. And see the beauty in that which is special and that which is not. Truth, like beauty, is not necessarily unique. It can also be in the everyday and the common.

> *Maybe. I think I've had enough of this conversation for now. It's time to wonder and wander. Time to see beautiful things. Or just have fun. Time to lighten up, old man.*

OK. But don't forget that it's your turn to make dinner. Don't forget the salt.

REFLECTION

1. How do you know when you belong somewhere?
   What makes a place special for you? What makes you
   feel special? Should you feel special?

2. When you're in a place where you feel as though you
   belong, what is it that you can do that you can't do
   in other places? How does being in a special place
   feel different?

3. What does it feel like to share your special place
   with other people? What are the things you share
   when you're in a place that you share with others?
   Why might it all start with belonging?

4. What do you need to do for other people to welcome
   you into their place? What are the things that you need
   to do to take care of a space you share with others?

NOTES

Part 2
Love

I enjoyed dinner last night – thank you.

> *You're welcome, old man. I've been wondering about something.*

Have you?

> *Yes. I need your help.*

How can I help?

> *Why do we love?*

That's a big question.

> *It is.*

Why do you think we love?

> *That's not fair. I asked first.*

I know.

> *You do this thing sometimes. It's annoying.*

I know.

I think it's good to have company most of the time. Sometimes it's good to be by yourself. Time to do things by yourself, test yourself out. Or just do nothing in particular. But company is pretty good most of the time.

Love is more than company.

I know that. It's much more than company. And it's not always a good thing.

Why's that?

Because it never stops. It never leaves you alone. And it doesn't always make you feel good. In fact, a lot of the time, love makes me feel angry.

Why angry?

Because it won't let go.

What doesn't it let go?

It doesn't let go of me. It doesn't make anything easy. It keeps demanding more.

A higher standard?

That's your words. For me, it's more like who I was yesterday doesn't matter much. Yesterday is done. Today is here, tomorrow's next and there's always something more to be done.

Why is that?

Because when you love someone, you don't want to let them down. But you know you will. Because you're not perfect. And you make mistakes.

Only mistakes?

> *Well, sometimes you also do things because you want to even though you know you shouldn't.*

Why do you think that is?

> *It's like you know you shouldn't, but it's fun to do something you shouldn't. At least it is in the moment. Then later, when you think about it, it's not.*

Complicated, isn't it?

> *Too right. And even if you know what's going to happen, you go out and do the selfish thing all over again. It'd be a whole lot easier if we didn't have all that stress. If we didn't have love, then we could just do what we wanted.*

Maybe. But what do you think would happen without love?

> *I think it'd be pretty good at first. You could do it all yourself. Do it your own way. Not have to worry about anyone or anything else.*

Then it'd get boring. And then it'd get lonely. You'd have to do everything yourself. Because no one would care enough to do anything for you. Particularly not the hard stuff.

> *So, when we love people, we do the hard stuff for them?*

Yes. For them or with them. Sometimes they don't even know that we're doing it. Or if they do, then they don't like it or even appreciate it.

> *You make love sound like a lot of hard work.*

It is. It's not easy. You keep getting it wrong.

I've heard you say things like that before. Is there anything you get right?

Sometimes. I don't know. Every now and then you do get it absolutely right. But even then, you have to keep going. Most of the time, you get some things right. Then you have to keep working on it when you'd rather be doing something else. Something easier.

It's a lot, isn't it, boy?

It is a lot. But the idea of life without love is worse. It's almost like you can't win.

Almost?

Well, it's pretty good, too. I mean, sometimes it's just the best. Nothing feels better than when you get love right. It's almost like we were made for it, made to be together and work it out.

Almost…

OK. Of course, we are meant to love. We are meant to find someone who can love us, and we can love them.

Only one person?

Well, one person seems to be the goal. One person with whom we can share our lives. But we love lots of people in our lives. There are friends, too. And family. We love them differently, of course.

What about people you don't know?

Oh, that's a hard question.

Think it through. You're doing well with love so far.

*How can you love someone you don't know? Don't you have
to know them first? Doesn't there have to be some kind of
chemistry between you?*

Chemistry can change.

*Oh, I know that! It can change and then you have to make a
choice: do I stick with it? Do I explore the new chemistry? Or
do I go somewhere else? And do I take the person with me?
Or should they be left behind for someone else?*

Maybe it's like this with people you don't know: we all need each
other. Otherwise, things would all fall apart. So, we have to work
out how we're going to keep it all together. We need to make the
chemistry work as best we can. We need rules to do that.

Are rules enough?

Maybe. Sometimes they're just what we need. And other times,
they're wrong. And we need to change them. Or get rid of them
altogether.

How would you know when to do that?

If you know people, then you know what's right and wrong for
them. Or at least you think you do. Until you don't. Until they
tell you. You need more than rules and knowledge. You need
understanding. You need…

Love?

Yes, you need love. But a different kind of love. You need to be
stronger because you have to find a way through in spite of people's
differences. You also need to be gentle with people's weaknesses.
You need to be able to forgive them for what they've done wrong.

And you need to be able to see the good in them, or at least the potential to be better.

Is that easy to do?

No, that's also hard. But then again, you'd want them to do the same for you, wouldn't you?

It's funny, isn't it? Love is something we can all share. Love and hate. But hate pulls us apart. We can hate something together, too. But in the end hate makes us more likely to hate everyone and everything.

Love makes us more likely to care for each other, to look after each other, to stay with each other. Love is like the glue that binds us to each other. It's so powerful, and not just for those with whom we're really close. It's almost like we were meant to live together. It's almost like we're meant to be in a community with each other.

Do you think you need a reason to love?

Well, yes. It makes sense, doesn't it? And not only is there a reason for love – love gives us a reason for each other. Love connects us. Love commits us to each other. Love keeps us going when times are tough. Love reminds us of what matters. Love rewards us.

But maybe love also doesn't need a reason. Maybe love just is. Maybe love just does what it does. Love delights us. Love brings us joy and sorrow in the moment and in the long term. Love motivates us. Love distracts us. Love reminds us. Love keeps us on track.

So, is love the reason?

I think it's always there in the reason. Or at least it should be. And if it's not, then you know you're off track.

Indeed. It's good to stay on track. Sometimes it's also good to go off track. As long as love takes you there. But not now. Let's keep going.

Yes. Let's do that.

REFLECTION

1. What does it mean to love and care for yourself? Is it right to love and care for yourself?

2. What are the types of love that you can feel for others? What makes them the same and what makes them different from each other? How do they make you feel?

3. How do people who love and care for each other show this to each other? Can this go wrong? How can you try to make it right when it's gone wrong?

4. Can you show love for people who you don't know? What might this look like?

NoTES

Part 3
Courage

It looks like we're almost there.

We're not.

But I can see the top, old man.

No. You can't.

No. I can see clear sky up ahead.

What you see is not always true or real. It feels that way, but feelings come and go. They have a particular power over us that speak to a need we have. The need is real, but the feeling can mislead us. You'll see.

How do you know that?

I've been here before. I've felt like you before.

Have you? When? With whom? What was it like?

It's not important now. Maybe another time.

But I want to know now.

Now is not the time.

Why not?

We have other things to think about and do now. The past is done already.

But…

Not now. Let's get to the top, then we can talk more.

That's not fair.

Fairness has nothing to do with it.

I don't believe you.

Yes, you do. You just don't want to admit it.

That's also unfair. I don't think you really know what it's like to be me. I don't feel you understand me.

Maybe. Maybe not. I understand enough to tell you what I know to be true, whether you like it or not. I understand that what's necessary in the moment might not be what seems fair to you.

I also understand that there's a false crest up ahead, the promise of something that will not be honoured now. That's also not fair. But it's real.

You're like a false crest sometimes.

That's unkind.

But it's real.

Yes. It's real. None of us ever really lives up to the promise. None of us is ever complete on our own. None of us can ever do all that's expected of us. It's the doubt. And the fear.

I'm not afraid.

Yes, you are. We all are. The greatest courage we can show is to own up to our fear. For when we are in the presence of our fear, we are revealed to ourselves and those around us for who we really are.

I'm not scared. I know we can make it to the top.

Then why do you sustain yourself with a false hope? Why do you tell yourself little lies to keep you going? It's better to see it and say it for what it is. Then, and only then, can you deal with it properly.

You're always so gloomy.

Perhaps not always.

More often than not.

I have seen things before. I understand what happens in our world.

You always go straight to the difficulties before you go to the other parts.

That's because the other parts are easy.

Well, sometimes it's good to do what is easy. It's fun.

Well, what's fun isn't always easy. It's fun to do what comes easily at first, but then it becomes boring. And it's not good to be bored.

No. It's not good to be bored. It's better to be busy, to be doing things. Except when it's not. Sometimes it's good just to do nothing.

Yes. You're right. But we can't always be like that.

> *No. We can't. Maybe you're right about fun, old man. Maybe there are different kinds of fun. There's the fun we have when we're doing nothing and the fun we have when we're doing something.*

That's very true.

> *I think the fun you have when you're doing something comes from getting things right. Sometimes that's easy and sometimes it's not. When it's not, it's good to think things through, to work out all the ways you might do something. To choose a way forward and give it a go. It feels good when you get it right.*

That's because of the promise you made yourself.

> *What promise is that?*

You tell me, boy.

> *Maybe it's about proving that you can do it. Maybe it's about looking at what scares you and facing it down.*

So, you do get scared…

> *Maybe.*

Maybe indeed. Maybe it's also about realising that you're not alone and that you can do it together.

> *Let's stop here and eat.*

Let's do that at the top. The view will be better there.

> *How do you know, old man?*

I have a feeling it will.

REFLECTION

1. What would you like to do in your life? What must you do in your life? How much choice and how much challenge do you think you should have?

2. Who helps you to become better at being you? What is it that they do for you? What do you do for them in return?

3. What story can you share with others? Can you tell a story of courage that can influence the choices that other people make? Can you inspire them to see that what's better lies ahead? Can you give them the direction they need and motivate them to meet and overcome their challenges?

4. What does it take to keep going, even when the challenge seems too great? What does it take to help other people to keep going, to grow in their strengths, to face their fears and to become better versions of themselves?

NOTES

NOTES

Part 4
Honesty

How far is there to go?

Today?

Yes, today.

As far as we can go.

And how far is that?

You need to ask a better question.

How much longer do we need to keep going?

That's not a better question.

When can we stop?

That's not a better question either.

What needs to be done today?

That's a better question. You need to learn to ask better questions to get better answers. We have things to do. We will keep going until they're done. We can take a break now. But not for too long. The day is short. And we have something to do.

Why does this thing need to be done?

Because it does.

That's not an honest answer.

Fair enough. But you didn't ask an honest question even if it was a better question. You didn't ask what you really want to know. You need to learn to ask better questions to get better answers. You need to learn to ask better and more honest questions to get better and more honest answers. What you want to know is why you have to do it, not why it needs to be done. If that's your better and more honest question, then ask it.

But know this: asking that better and more honest question will not change what needs to be done. What needs to be done needs to be done. You can't turn it into something else or make it go away by asking a wrong and dishonest question. You can't change what is real and true by asking a wrong and dishonest question. Whatever you ask, this thing must still be done. It will stay the same and must still be done, and you must play your part in getting it done.

And even when it is done, it of itself will not have changed. It will be you that must change – you and how you look at what must be done. You can work out a better way to get it done. And you can work out what you can do about getting it done this better way. This will mean asking questions that are both better and more honest.

But asking better and more honest questions will still not change what must be done. It's not the thing that needs doing that will change when you learn to ask better and more honest questions. It will always be you. And so, after you learn to ask better and more honest questions, you will also need to become more ready to listen to better and more honest answers that you won't like.

Working out how you change to respond better and more honestly to the answers that present themselves to you is your next task. What will you change about yourself to listen, to learn and to get done what must be done?

> *Why must it be done? Why do we need to do it? Why do I need to do it? There's too much to do. And I don't want to do it.*

What you say is better and more honest. When you ask 'why?' in this way, you really ask for a reason why this thing must be done now and why you must do this instead of doing something else you think you want to do now. There's always too much to do in the here and now. And never enough time. And always something else we could do instead.

Put simply, we must do this thing because we chose to do what was needed to be done when we set out together. And so, we must do this thing. We must do what we can today. We must do it now. Sometimes, that is a reason why we must do what we can and must that is clear from the start. Sometimes, a reason becomes clear along the way. Sometimes, we get to the end and we are still asking what the point of it all was.

> *What's the point of that? Can't we do something else?*

Perhaps. But not today. Today we are doing this thing. And we must do it – or at least all of it that we can. We must keep going until all that we can do is done. Because we chose to do this. When we made this choice, we knew it was the right thing to do. Even if we doubt this now, it is still the right thing to do.

For it has not changed. So, what has changed? Have we changed our minds about it? And if so, why have we changed our minds? Why do we doubt what is real and true? If we truly doubt this thing, and if it is indeed worth doubting, the time will come when it is clear that we can and should do something else instead. But before that can happen, we must be sure that we do not mistake doubting the thing for doubting ourselves.

Right now, I do not doubt what must be done, boy. And although you question it, you do not doubt that what must be done is real and true and right. In truth, you really don't want to do it because you doubt that you can do it. And there is only one way to deal with this doubt.

You can and must do this thing. In doing it, you may come to find a reason that is not about you. Even if you do not, you will come to see what is real and true and right about you: that you are needed to do this thing. That, more than anything else right now, is why you are here. You are needed until it is done. And you can and must go ahead and do it now before you give in to your doubt.

I don't like that answer.

That's both a better and more honest response. But it doesn't change what must be done.

We've stopped for long enough. We must do this thing. We must do what we can now. You will see. Break's over. Pick yourself up and let's go, boy.

OK. But I still don't like that answer, old man.

REFLECTION

1. How honest are you with yourself? Are you too hard on yourself? Do you soften the truth to make life easier?

2. What is a reputation? Why is it important to have a good reputation? How can you work with others to build a reputation for being both reliable and fair?

3. How can you encourage others to be truthful when times are tough?

4. How can you build a deep and abiding understanding with other people about what is true in life? How can you help each other to do the good and right thing by being honest with each other?

NOTES

NOTES

Part 5
Joy

I don't like it still and I am tired, old man.

Enough of the 'old man' thing.

Can't take a joke?

When you say it like that, it's no joke. You mean it. And you're being mean when you say it. So, no more talking today. Do not tell me any more of your troubles in this moment. I have heard enough of them from you. I know them and I know you. This is a time to be with your own thoughts.

Choose your own path. Set your own pace. Eat, drink and sleep as you will. Work through your anger. Turn to what is good in you and let it come to the fore. Breathe. Breathe slowly. Breathe slowly and deeply in time with the movement of your feet, your arms and the rest of your body.

Feel your feet as they make contact with the ground. Feel your connection to what is around you, to all creatures, all living things, all of the Earth. Feel your footsteps and the change they bring with them, so step down with care to protect from harm and step up with the confidence that you can make a difference for the better.

Listen to the world around you. Listen to the sound of your breathing, the rise and fall of your lungs, the in and out of the air. Taste the air, the water, the sweat on your lips. Spend time with the view.

Think back to what you said about love. You are important to me; but you are not nearly as important to the world as you think you are. There is so much else in the world, so much else to encounter, so much else to take in. There is so much else to do.

Take pleasure. Take pleasure in who you are becoming and the person you have left behind.

Find beauty. Find beauty in the presence of the other and the blooming of a rare and delicate relationship that will reveal the depth and breadth of what you might yet give.

Receive joy. Receive joy because you are needed for your precious love and the work you must do to offer yourself wholly and completely.

I will be here. I will walk beside you in silence today. And tomorrow, we will sit and look each other in the eyes. We will talk again, and I will rejoice as you tell me how you have grown.

REFLECTION

1. What does it mean to have fun? How do you feel when
    you're having fun in the moment? How do you know
    when other people are sharing in your fun?

2. Can you tell a joke? What's it like to tell a joke and have
    other people laugh at it? What's the difference between
    'telling' a joke and 'making' a joke out of something
    or someone else? What happens when other people
    tell you that what you thought was only a joke was
    something else, something more hurtful to them?

3. What can fun do that's helpful? When does fun get
    in the way? What happens when you delay the fun?
    What happens when you help others to look beyond
    the fun in the moment to search for and find other
    things of value?

4. How can you take on a challenge and find joy in
    overcoming it? What does this joy feel like when you
    find it and share it with others?

NOTES

NOTES

Part 6
Grace

I'm sorry. I should have tried harder.

I'm not sure you could have tried harder than you did.

Yes, maybe. I could have been better, though. I could have been a better version of me.

Yes, you could have. But now you are. It just took a little time for you to find the character to get there. It's all part of the grace of being in the world.

Thank you. It did. But I couldn't have got there without you.

Thank you. It's what I'm meant to do. You've learned a lot. And I couldn't have got here without you, too. Did you sleep well? Can I get you something to eat?

No, I didn't sleep well, but I will tonight. Let me make you something. I'm enjoying doing this thing with you. I think I'm growing stronger. I'm learning more about the thoughts that become the actions that become the habits that help us tell our story. I'm writing it all down in my book: that's what I'm meant to do.

What have you written down?

> *Everything that matters. It's a story. About character.*
> *You can read it while you eat.*

Then we should go back. We're ready now. We've done what we came to do.

> *But first, can you pass the salt? asked the younger man.*
> *It'll give the food more flavour.*

OK. I'll read while you cook.

"Come with me, the man said," read the older man.

REFLECTION

1. What is your character? What are your strengths? How do you know when you have grown in your character?

2. Why can it be hard for you to forgive? How can you show your forgiveness to others? What does it take to move on from a difficult moment between you and someone else? How can you find and share fun, challenge and joy again?

3. What is reciprocity? Why is it important? How do we show reciprocity to and with others?

4. What might be the character of a life that is worthwhile and well lived? Is the purpose of this life more likely to be about the pursuit of your own gain or the service of others? How will you tell the story of the journey you've taken together?

NOTES

NOTES

Epilogue
A Life of Purpose

Each of us is on a journey.

My journey began in 1969. As a father, grandfather, partner, writer, historian, professor and teacher, I've been trying to work out a way forward and tell the story of the pathway I have taken since then. I've had many adventures and hope to have had a few more before my time is done.

My family has been a very important part of both my journey and my story. Perhaps I'll tell you more about them another time. For the moment, it's important to me that you know they have been part of the story in this book, *A Journey*. Some of the conversations in the book have their origins in conversations I have had (or wanted to have) with family members.

The illustrations in this book have been drawn by two members of my family. The picture at the start of this Epilogue is of me when I was 15 and was drawn by my father, Dr Brian Patrick Cummins. A very accomplished artist, he didn't draw and paint me often, but I really treasure this one. The pictures at the start of each of the other chapters have been drawn especially for this book by my very talented niece, Maia Jelavic, who is completing the same

Fine Arts degree at the very same campus that her grandfather
did many years ago. I'm very lucky to have such talent and such
illustrations to amplify my words.

Everything you have read and seen in this story about a journey is
meant for you. It's drawn from deep reserves of passion and insight
that have come from the heads and hearts of students (and those
who teach, care for, lead and love them) all over the world as they
told me about what, how and why they want to build a life that is
both worthwhile and well lived.

Over many years, what young people across the globe have told
me is that they want to connect with something more. They want
to be part of something that goes beyond their own emotional,
intellectual and physical selves. They have told me that they want
to embark on a journey of exploration and discovery. They want to
encounter self-awareness, relationship, service and a vocation that
takes them beyond self-interest towards selflessness.

They know already that a life of giving to others is transformative
for each of us. This is because it's grounded in the genuine
meaningfulness that equips us to tell our story, that empowers us to
test what's possible, and that enables us to make a difference. They
want to make this difference. They want the opportunity to be and
become this difference.

So, what will make a difference in your life? What will help you
lead a good life? What will bring you a life that's both worthwhile
and well lived?

It's all about a life of purpose.

A life of purpose is about claiming a fundamental reason for
everything that you do in your life and then going out and doing it.

It means you can actually do the things that really matter – it's your most powerful reason 'why?'.

What does it mean to live with purpose?

When you commit to learn, live, lead and work through a life of purpose, you engage in a process of becoming a better version of yourself, of growing in character.

Discovering what your purpose might be and how you might learn, live, lead and work in pursuit of it requires you to embark on a personal journey of inquiry, exploration, discovery and encounter that will help you to form the character, competency and wellness to thrive in the world. I call this journey The Pathway to Excellence.

It starts with four fundamental questions that will help you to develop your character – the way you live your life and wrestle with the inner drive to realise yourself while replicating the external expectations of others:

1. Who am I?

2. Where do I fit in?

3. How can I best serve others?

4. Whose am I?

This is an ongoing, inside-out process of being, becoming and transformation that can help you to both experience and contribute through a life of purpose. It's about helping you to grow, make progress, achieve and succeed.

To continue to grow in mastery on The Pathway to Excellence, therefore, you will need to commit to a regular program of reflecting on who you have been, who you are and who you are becoming – your yesterday, today and tomorrow – and the purpose to which this journey is increasingly being dedicated. You will have seen reflections throughout this little book. I hope you have found them helpful as the different stages unfolded.

As you think about whether you might want to commit to a program of asking and answering these questions, I have a few more for you that might help you to come to know your purpose and see it realised in the journey of your lifetime: the building of your character.

1. **Discover: How am I showing my character?**

    - *What does good character look like to me?*

    - *What actions do I take to show this character?*

    - *How do I share my character at its best with others?*

2. **Diagnose: What am I learning about myself as a person of character?**

    - *What's one thing that I'm doing well that I want to become even better at?*

    - *What's one thing that I'm not doing well that I want to improve?*

    - *What's something that I'm not doing now that I might like to try?*

3. **Decide: What changes do I want to make in who I'm becoming?**

    - *What differences do I want to see in myself?*

    - *What do I want to leave as is?*

    - *What goals might I set to become stronger in my character?*

4. **Design: What's my plan to bring about these changes?**

    - *What steps could I take to achieve my goals?*

    - *When could I realistically do these things?*

    - *What would success look like?*

5. **Deploy: What support do I need to make this happen?**

    - *Is there anything I need that I don't have in place right now?*

    - *Who can help me achieve my goals?*

    - *How can I get this help?*

You can use these questions any day of any week to think about where you have come from, where you are now and where you might go next. The answers to them will help you frame your story of yesterday, today and tomorrow.

What a story that could be!

Your journey awaits.

I'm excited.

I can't wait.

Let's go!

Phil

www.ingramcontent.com/pod-product-compliance
Lightning Source LLC
Chambersburg PA
CBHW071841190726

48292CB00005B/1869